MATHU TARU!

MARA MATHA PAR MUK!

MATHU KHAI CHE!

MARA MATHA PAR!

MATHU TARU!

MARA MATHA PAR MUK!

MATHU NA KHA!

MARA MATHA PAR MUK!

MARA MATHA PAR MUK!

MATHU
TARU!

MARA MATHA
PAR MUK!

MATHU
KHAI CHE!

MARA
MATHA
PAR!

MATHU
TARU!

MARA MATHA
PAR MUK!

MATHU
NA KHA!

MARA MATHA
PAR MUK!

PUT IT ON MY HEAD!

MARA MATHA PAR MUK!

BY SIMMI PATEL

PAPER SAMOSA

ISBN: 9798494825926

FOR THE LOVE

OF BAA!

♡

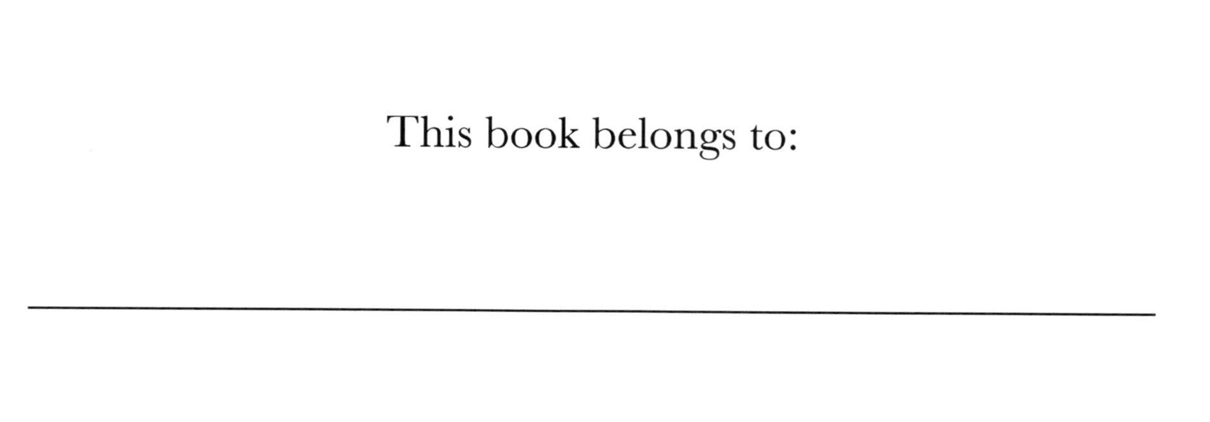
This book belongs to:

BAA!

WHERE DOES THIS BALL GO?

MARA
MATHA
PAR!

TULSI
BAA!
WHERE IS THE
WATERING CAN?

MARA MATHA PAR!

BAA!

WHERE SHOULD
I BUILD MY
SAREE FORT?

ON MY HEAD!

MARA MATHA PAR!

BAA!
WHERE SHOULD I PUT THE RICE?

PUT IT ON MY HEAD!

MARA MATHA PAR MUK!

BAA!
WHAT'S FOR DINNER??

CALL
1-800-NO-DBSR
COUPON
PIZZA DELIVERY
1-800-NO-DBSR

MY HEAD!

MARU MATHU!

BAA!
I WANT TO
GET A DOG!

YOUR HEAD!
MATHU TARU!

BAA!

WHAT ABOUT
A CAT?

DON'T EAT MY HEAD!

MATHU NA KHA!

BAA!
BAA!
BAA!
BAA!!!

YOU'RE EATING MY HEAD!
MATHU KHAI CHE!

BUT
BAA!
I GOT YOU THIS!
WHERE SHALL I
PUT IT?
#1 BAA

PUT IT ON MY HEAD!

MARA MATHA PAR MUK!

I LOVE YOU, BAA
#1 BAA
I LOVE YOU TOO, BETA!

THE
END!

NOW GO
TO SLEEP!

♡

SUY JA
HAVÉ

A NOTE FROM THE AUTHOR

I have so much fun translating my experiences, ideas, and silly musings into art and writing. Thank you so much for allowing me to share my stories with you!

Love,

Simmi Patel
Creator of Paper Samosa

@paper.samosa

www.papersamosa.com

MATHU TARU!

MARA MATHA PAR MUK!

MATHU KHAI CHE!

MATHU KHAI CHE!

MARA MATHA PAR!

ATHA UK!

MAR MATH PAR

MATHU TARU!

THU KHA!

MARA MATHA PAR MUK!

MATHU NA KHA!

MATHA UK!

MARA MA PAR MUK

MARA MATHA PAR MUK!

MARA MATHA

MATHU TARU